SO MUCH POTENTIAL

A Best Books for Kids & Teens * Starred * Selection

BOOKS BY THIS AUTHOR

Phoebe Sproule Novels:

8 Days in DUMBO

The Haunting of Cedar Hill Plantation

The Complete Babysitter Out of Control! Series:

Babysitter Out of Control!

Looking For Love on Mongo Tongo

The Improbable Party on Purple Plum Lane

What Happened in July

The Sinking of the Wiley Bean

The Queen of Second Chances

And:

So Much Potential

Carried Away on Licorice Days

Margaret J. McMaster

SO MUCH POTENTIAL

Mansbridge Dunn Publishers

ISBN: 978-0-9810525-7-1

The author gratefully acknowledges the support of the Ontario Arts Council in the writing of this book.

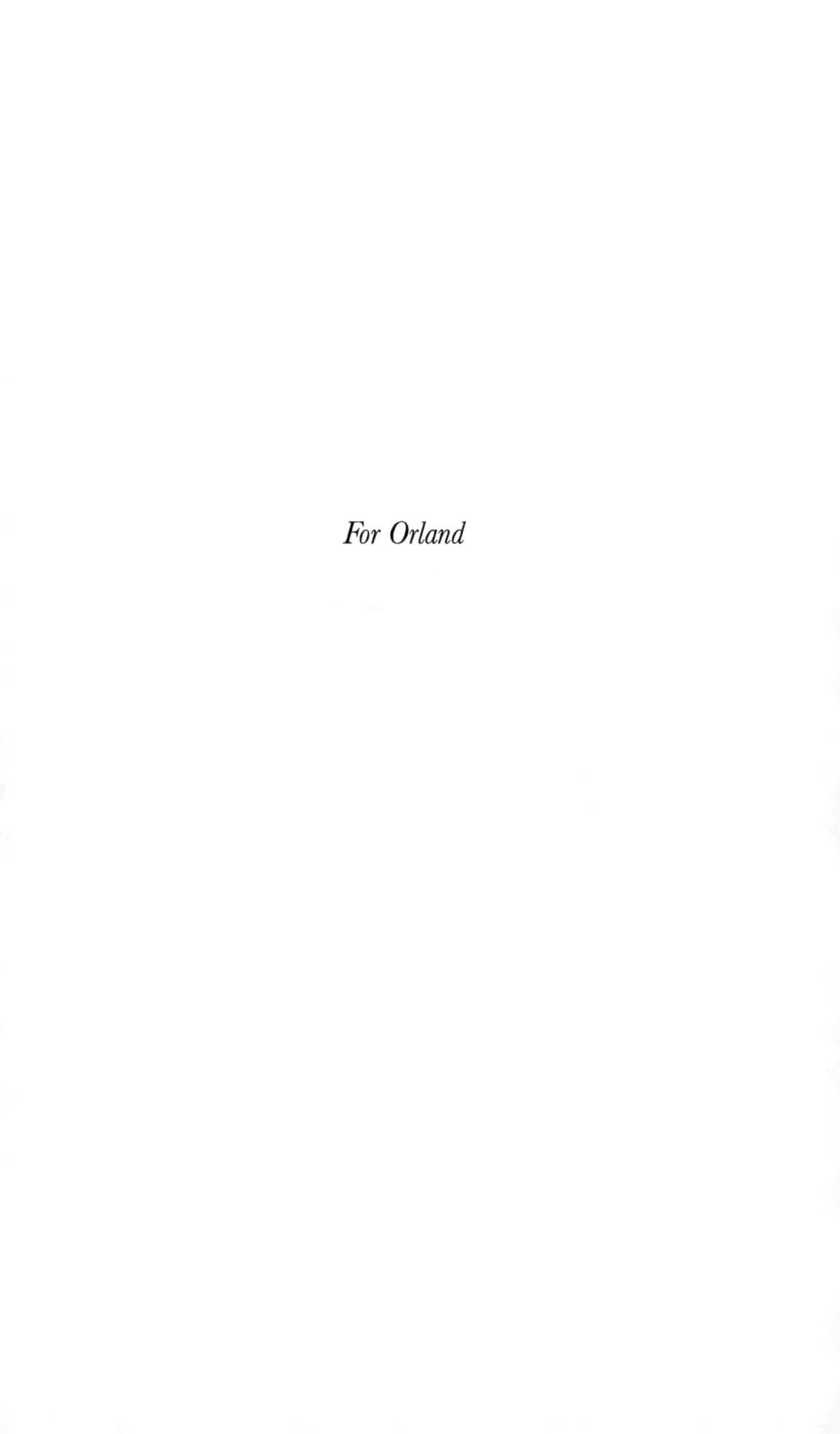

For Orland

CHAPTER 1

This is what I'd like to tell everyone who thinks I've got it made because my father's a doctor and brings in the big bucks: it comes with its own set of baggage.

A pocket guide to our family: there are expectations. Mostly Dad's. They involve getting a lot of initials after my name.

'You might as well kill me now,' I say to him, 'because I'm going to die if you stick me in front of a pile of books and make me memorize a lot of long words for the next ten years.'

He comes back with: 'Other kids would kill for your opportunities.'

'So, put some other kid through university. Lots of them need help. Look at me, Dad. Really look at me. It's not what I want. I want to be on the lake before dawn and have a catch on ice by noon. I want to play a round of golf or take my kids (fictional at this point) to the park in the afternoon.'

'Anybody who gets the marks you do,' he huffs. 'Is that what you're going to do with the rest of your life? Fish?'

'I get it, Dad. All the other dads are talking about their kids' plans and I'm an embarrassment, aren't I? I bet you haven't even said the words out loud: My son wants to be a fisherman.'

I've struck a chord. I can tell by the look on his face.

'Dad, I'm not trying to humiliate you with my choice. I just don't want to work myself into an ulcer for a life I don't care about.'

Deep sigh. Some muttering about how I've been spoiled.

'No, just the opposite. Having a lot of things doesn't do it for me. If I never have a huge house and a Mercedes, I'll be fine.'

'Which is just another way of saying that you have no ambition.'

I'm dumbstruck by this. 'Dad, I *have* ambitions.'

'*Really?* What are they?'

'Why are you being sarcastic?'

'Sorry. What are your ambitions?'

'I want to be captain of my own tug some day, with a crew, and the largest quota on the lake. That's not a small thing.'

He takes off his glasses and rubs his eyes. 'It's just … if you don't go to university now, you probably never will. And you've got so much potential.'

'We're going in circles,' I say.

CHAPTER 2

Whatever they're doing to bring the lake back to life, it's working. I should know. I'm working at the Assessment Plant, running fish through the scaling machine.

A guy named Dylan mans the forklift. He's in his late thirties and thinks he was called to fishing by Jesus. 'Who were the first disciples?' he asks me. 'Fishermen. Good, honest, hardworking fishermen.'

Dylan crewed on a tug for fifteen years, the best years of his life until the day his boot got caught in the nets as they soared to the bottom of the lake. He offered this desperate prayer as he was being dragged underwater: 'I'll be a good man and devote my life to your service, if only …'

And then, according to Dylan, Lake Erie's mythical monster, South Bay Bessie, a relic of a prehistoric age with a body forty feet long, tore through the net and freed him. Unfortunately, she also separated him from part of his foot. As a result, that was his last day crewing a tug. Now he picks up the totes of fish left on the dock when the boats come in and runs them into the plant where I work.

I like Dylan because no matter what life throws at him, he stays positive. He also let me stay at his place when dad kicked me out of the house.

'A 90% average, four years in a row, and your dad kicked you out of the house?' he says, scratching his head. 'What's up with that?'

For those of you who've been kicked out of the house for more significant reasons, it may sound a little weird. For Dad, it was a natural reflex.

Everything came to a head when Queen's University accepted me into its pre-med program. I'd applied just to keep him happy - but when I tossed my acceptance letter into the garbage, he blew a fuse.

By contrast, Mom doesn't care if I become a juggler. She left Dad ranting and raving in the family room and followed me upstairs.

'Give him time to cool down,' she says. 'He'll come around.'

'No, Mom. There's no way he can have his way and I can have mine.'

She nods, knowing what a control freak he is. 'You've both got the same temper, you know.'

'Yeah, Mom, you've told me that before.'

'But, you've got his brains too,' she adds.

I look at her stonily. 'Fishermen have brains.'

'Of course they do,' she says. 'And they need them. You'll be a great one.'

I pause for a moment and some of the steam goes out of me. 'You mean that?'

'Of course, I do.'

'What about Dad's dreams of me becoming a doctor?'

'Oh *please*,' she scoffs. 'Kids who want to be doctors are a dime a dozen. How many want to be fishermen?'

You gotta love a mother like that.

So, I leave on good terms with my mother, and bad terms with my father, and end up living in Dylan's tiny apartment over the liquor store with his chocolate lab, Boz.

Dylan is still puzzled by it. 'He kicked you out because you don't want to go to university? I don't get it.'

CHAPTER 3

Al and Cruddy, the two guys working with me on the scaling machine, have limited options. As far as they're concerned, scaling fish beats detasselling corn or working in one of the greenhouses. There's a roof over their heads and it's cool even on the hot and muggy days.

In the beginning they gave me the business about being a poor, misunderstood rich kid, but my status went up when they saw me 'standing up to the man'. To be honest, I was heartbroken when Dad kicked me out, but these aren't guys you talk to about heartbreak.

Mom comes to the plant and brings me a sandwich, which I eat on my break. 'Not a word about this to your father,' she says.

Dad thinks that a summer on the dock will cure me of the whole fishing thing. Mom told him not to be so sure.

All this for some stinkin' fish, you ask?

No. All this for a life on the lake.

CHAPTER 4

When the winds are strong and the lake is choppy, the boats don't go out. When the boats don't go out, there's no fish. When there's no fish, there's no work, simple as that. Our supervisor, Tim, sends us home. I figure Dad's at work, so I go home.

I stuff my dirty clothes into the washer with a capful of detergent and while that's churning away I dig out a backpack and cram more underwear and socks into it. In the hour it takes for the load to finish, I lie on my bed and fall asleep.

Sometime later, when I feel my shoulder being shaken, I'm so far under I don't know where I am. I bang Mom on the forehead as I catapult myself out of bed.

'Ow,' she cries.

'Sorry.'

She eyeballs me to see if I'm sick, which I'm obviously not, then says, 'Why aren't you at work?'

My voice is thick from sleep. 'The boats didn't go out.'

'Oh.' She spots the backpack on the floor. 'What are you doing? Stealing the silver?'

'We have silver?'

She waits until I'm on my feet before she suggests lunch. 'Are you hungry? I can whip up some scrambled eggs and toast.'

I switch my clothes to the dryer and sit down at the kitchen table. The heap of scrambled eggs Mom sets down in front of me slides down pretty fast.

'Hmmm,' she says. 'What about a milkshake? That should fill you up.'

She makes it with chocolate sauce and real ice cream. I wonder if Al or Cruddy have ever tasted a real milkshake. I doubt it. All the fast food restaurants make it from a mix.

'Penny for your thoughts,' she says.

I gulp down the shake and say, 'I was thinking about the guys that work with me. They're not much older than I am but they're pretty much on their own. They don't seem to have much backup.'

She clears the dishes from the table. 'That's too bad.'

A few minutes later she's banging pots and pans around.

'What are you doing?' I ask.

'Making a lasagna for your dad's dinner,' she replies. 'It's his favourite.'

Right then I realize that Mom doesn't understand the first thing about making a stand. I'm about to mention this when she says, 'Even pig-headed fools have to eat.'

CHAPTER 5

The next day the weather is better and the boats come in loaded with pickerel and yellow perch. Al and Cruddy and I push the fish through the scaler as fast as we can. When it's break time Al goes out for a smoke and I pop a can of Coke with Cruddy in the lunchroom.

Cruddy is a plain-faced lump of a guy. I've worked with him for a month now and he's barely said two words to me. Today he wants to know if I've got any money.

I screw up my face. 'What kind of money? Are you talking about a loonie for the Coke machine or money for a new car?'

His eyes light up. 'You've got that much?'

'Seriously, Cruddy? I'm living hand to mouth right now. How much do you need?'

His face falls. 'Never mind.'

'No, really. Talk to me.'

He hunches his head between his shoulders and stares at the table and I know I'm not going to get anything more out of him.

The last tug reaches the wharf by noon and by three o'clock we've got the day's catch scaled and run up the hill to the Processing Plant to be filleted.

I'm halfway to the gym on my bike when I realize that I've left my gym bag in my locker. I turn back on the lake road and coast down the hill to the dock. The tugs are bobbing in their berths and the dock is deserted. Suddenly I hear a loud splash to my right. I look in that direction but the only thing that catches my eye is a freighter coming through the channel to unload gravel.

When I finally get to the gym I spend an hour on weights and another on the spin bike. I'm dripping with sweat when Lacey (my girlfriend, ex-girlfriend, girlfriend, ex-girlfriend) comes in. She takes a whiff of me and says, 'You stink, fish boy.'

Lacey is smart and gorgeous and dating the school quarterback, Dexter. Right from the beginning she laid it out to Dexter, who's a bit of a cocky wiener, that she'd be hanging out with me whenever she felt like it. Then she told him she was going to beauty school to get her certification, not following him to university, so, if he had any issues, he could shove off. So far he hasn't, but I hear that long distance relationships are killers.

Lacey has her own beauty shop in the laundry room of her house. Most of the girls at school get their hair done there because she charges half what the salons do.

'What are you doing here?' I ask.

She punches me in the arm and says, 'I thought *you'd* be here. I just had a steam.' She brushes hair off her face. 'You hungry? I brought some spaghetti and garlic bread.'

Suddenly I get it. 'You heard dad kicked me out, didn't you?'

She rolls her eyes. 'Are you kidding me? The beauty shop is gossip central.'

I towel the sweat off my face. 'Anybody on my side?'

'I hate to break it to you, Andy, but everyone thinks you're a doofus.'

'Thanks.'

'You're welcome.'

'What do you think?'

'I'm not a good one to ask. I'd trample my mother to live in your house.' She looks at the spin bike. 'Are you finished here?'

'Yeah. I just need to grab a shower.'

'Okay, meet me upstairs.'

By the time I get upstairs Lacey has set out a feast on one of the tables. Technically, the eating area is for people drinking the gym's protein shakes so I'm not surprised to see a guy from our school on his way over to talk to us. Wendell is six foot two and on the football team with Dexter. I don't want to take him on.

'Hi guys,' he says, in a friendly way.

Lacey looks at him and bats her eyelashes but somehow I don't think that's going to work with Wendell.

'Just so you know,' he says, 'this area is off limits for take-out.'

'Good to know,' Lacey says. 'We'll try not to take anything out.'

Wendell blushes. 'You know what I mean.'

Lacey tries her best to look confused. 'Oh,' she says, 'I thought you said take-out.'

Wendell isn't buying it, and I have an uneasy feeling that I'm going to be called in to intervene.

'Don't make me call management,' he says. 'I've told you nicely.'

Lacey switches tactics and points her garlic bread at his head. 'And don't make me tell everyone at school that you have to sleep with the light on, Wendell.'

I know this must be true because Wendell slinks back to wherever it was he came from and Lacey continues dishing spaghetti out of the Tupperware.

'Do you want parmesan?' she asks, as though nothing happened. I look around uneasily for Wendell but he's nowhere to be seen.

Lacey and I don't talk again until we've finished eating and she's packed everything away in her gym bag. Then she gets serious and says, 'You've got to go home, Andy.'

My voice changes octaves. 'What? I can't.'

'Yes, you can. And you've got to do it soon.'

'Why? Dad's being completely unreasonable.'

'I get it. You're trying to make a point, he's trying to make a point. But there's no upside to being the troubled-family-of-the-month in this town.'

I find it very annoying when she's right.

'What if he doesn't want me there?' I ask, rather pitifully.

She looks at me as though I'm incapable of figuring anything out for myself and says, 'I can have a talk with him, if you want.'

God, that girl has balls. I think when I first realized that, I had to break up with her.

We pass Wendell on our way out. Lacey gives him a thumbs-up to let him know he's safe and he grins at her gratefully.

CHAPTER 6

When I tell Dylan that I'm moving back home he grins from ear to ear. Later, I find out that the guys had a bet on.

The next morning Cruddy doesn't show up for work. Tim comes down from the office and asks if we know where he is.

'Maybe he's sick,' Al says.

Tim wrinkles his forehead. 'Too sick to call in?'

We shrug and look dumb, which is the only way we can look because we don't know anything.

With a man short we have to work like stink to keep up. When we're finally able to take a break I follow Al outside. He lights a cigarette and takes a long draw off it.

'You don't smoke?' he says on the exhale.

I shake my head. 'No, never.'

We sit and look mindlessly out at the water as the fishing tug, Bonnie Belle, pulls into its berth. Al points his cigarette at it and says, 'That's a bad one.' I squint to see what he's talking about. 'Something's wrong in the head with that guy.'

'Who? The captain?'

'Yeah.'

I wait for him to fill me in on the details, but after a few minutes I realize he's had second thoughts. He takes a final puff of his cigarette and butts it out. The break ends and we go back to the scaling machine.

CHAPTER 7

The next day the OPP come to the plant because Cruddy's not just AWOL, Cruddy is *missing*. 'Stupid bugger,' Al says.

Tim comes out and calls us into his office.

The policemen who question us are as solid as Hummers. The bald one looks at me and says, 'What can you tell us about your co-worker Malcolm Sewell?'

'Who?'

'Cruddy,' Tim says.

'Oh.'

I tell them I don't know very much. How could I? I didn't even know his real name.

'How long have you been working here?'

'A month.'

'Summer job?'

'No, it's the start of my career path.'

The cops exchange looks.

'You bein' smart?'

'No.'

'Aren't you Doc Towell's kid?' the other one asks.

I tell him I am and he immediately gives me that 'what a doofus' look. The bald guy scribbles something in his notepad and says, 'Do you have any idea where Malcolm is?'

I shake my head. 'Not a clue.' Suddenly I remember. 'But, a couple of days ago he asked me for money.'

He writes this down. 'Did you give him any?'

'No. I'm pretty broke myself right now.'

'What did he need it for?'

'I don't know.'

'Did he say he was going somewhere?'

'Why? Do you think something's happened to him?'

'We're not making any assumptions at this point,' he says. 'These guys usually turn up.'

Dead or alive, I wanted to ask, but didn't.

CHAPTER 8

I want to crew on a tug but the only time I can talk to the ship captains is before they head out in the morning. Dylan's not too happy when I roll off the couch at 4:00 a.m. and wake up Boz.

'When did you say you were moving out?' he says, groggily.

I make my way gingerly down the stairwell to the street. It's a two-minute ride to the dock on my bike and when I get there it's alive with sleepy women dropping off their husbands.

I stop at the TPR Enterprise first because I know the captain, Don Fletcher. He coached me in soccer when I was little. One day after practice he brought the whole team out and showed us his boat. He's the reason I want to be a fisherman.

Don's surprised to see me climbing up into the wheelhouse.

'Andy, what are you doing here?' he asks.

'Looking for work, actually.'

'Here?'

'Yeah, I've been working in the plant since school finished but I want to get out on the lake.'

'You know I don't hire summer help,' he says. 'The season's too long.'

'I know. I'm looking for something permanent.'

He looks at me skeptically. 'You're not going back to school?'

'No, I want to be a fisherman. That's my long-term plan. And I'd like to work for you.'

He looks in his side view mirror. The crew's on board and it's time to get the tug out.

'I may have something for you next week,' he says. 'One of my guys is having surgery and he's going to be off for a couple of months. If you prove yourself …'

I thank him and disembark just before the crew casts off. The Enterprise slips through the harbour and disappears into the black lake. I know Dylan will kill me if I wake him up again so I spend the next couple of hours at Tim Hortons.

~

Our job scaling fish doesn't require special skills so Cruddy is easy to replace. The new guy, Jake, turns out to be his exact opposite. He talks all day long, mostly about TV reality shows. I have no idea what he's talking about so I nod at everything he says.

At three o'clock Lacey comes down to the dock to pick me up. She's been up to Dylan's and has my stuff in her car. Normally the guys would wolf-whistle a dish like Lacey, but they restrain themselves because she's with me.

Dad's not home when we roll in but Mom's watching the little television set she has mounted on the kitchen wall. She shushes us before we even say anything and points to the screen.

Lacey and I turn our eyes to the breaking news. There are police cars and satellite news trucks and people gawking from the side of the road. The journalist covering the story is almost hysterical with excitement. He breathlessly reports that they've found the car belonging to the young man missing for almost a week.

Mom motions to a pot of coffee on the stove. I look at Lacey to see if she wants any but she ignores me. 'Isn't that by the Point?' she says. 'Where those dinky cottages are?'

I watch as the camera pans over the scene. 'I think you're right. I wonder what Cruddy was doing up there?'

Mom shushes us again, but the reporter is just filling in time so she switches the set off. 'Your father's going to be late for dinner. Do you want me to make you a sandwich to tide you over?'

'Okay, sure.'

'What about you, Lacey?' she asks.

Lacey says she's sorry but she's got someone coming in for highlights and has to go.

CHAPTER 9

A week later Don stops by the Assessment Plant and tells me I can start work on the Enterprise the next morning. Tim's annoyed at having to get someone to fill my job but tells me to take my oil skins and gloves until I can get my own.

Four guys crew the boat deck. Don rarely leaves the wheelhouse. The first thing he explains to me is the pay. He takes fifty percent of the catch; the other fifty percent is split between the crew. He advises me to have some money saved up for when the catch is poor. Then he introduces me to the guys I'll be working with: Larry, Mike, and Scottie. They fill me in on the rest as we motor out to the nets.

First, they tell me about the fish. Yellow perch, pickerel, and whitefish, have quotas. Don has bought some of these quotas, others he has leased. This year he's allowed to pull in 600,000 pounds of fish. Before the quotas, tugs could run two crews, 24 hours a day. With today's technology it'd be very easy to fish out the lake, so the quotas seem like a good thing.

Some fish, like white perch, white bass, and smelt, don't have quotas, but you have to trawl for smelt so Don doesn't bother with them. We send down gill nets that rest at the bottom of the lake. A series of buoys, with the TPR Enterprise colours, mark where they are. Don also records the location in his log book, although the nets drift a bit with the current.

As soon as we get to the buoys, we haul up the nets using an hydraulic lifter. We pack the fish in insulated totes under layers of crushed ice then drop the nets back down. My job consists of untangling the fish that are stuck in the nets. I work with something like a crochet hook but the fish slip and slide through my gloves. The guys say I put on a pretty good show.

As soon as the fish are on ice we set out to the next location and repeat the process, until, by the end of the day, we've pulled up four miles of net.

I don't touch any of my sandwiches until I see Larry unwrap a donut, then I practically devour one whole.

Mike pours coffee from a thermos and looks out at the grey sky. 'We're going to get some rain,' he says. The other guys nod in agreement and pass the thermos around. When we finish our midmorning snack we take turns peeing in a bucket, the only washroom on board.

Every muscle in my body aches when I get home and I'm thankful I'm not sleeping on Dylan's couch anymore. I tell Mom I'll need twice as much food tomorrow then drag my weary body upstairs. I crash before I can even take a shower.

CHAPTER 10

I wake up to the buzzing of the alarm clock and eat breakfast alone: stick-to-the-ribs oatmeal, a bowl of fruit, and six slices of raisin toast. Then I ease myself quietly out the door.

It's very dark as Don steers the Enterprise into the lake. There are mattresses laid out behind him in the wheelhouse and because there isn't anything to do for the next hour I decide to catch some sleep. When I awake, the sky has transformed from inky black to pale grey and I can hear the guys cursing on the deck below me.

'What's going on?' I ask as I make my way downstairs.

Mike points to the buoys bobbing in the lake and says, 'Some blasted idiot's put his nets over ours.' Larry mutters the words 'Bonnie Belle' under his breath.

If you're lazy and unscrupulous enough you can let someone else scout out the fish, then take advantage of it. When we do get our catch up, it's about half of what it should be. This, of course, will affect our paycheques, which is why the men are bitter.

As soon as the meagre haul is on ice, Don comes down from the wheelhouse to talk to Mike about moving our nets. I'm staring into the murky water, not thinking about anything in particular, when, suddenly, a long shadow flashes by under the surface.

'Did you see that?' I ask Larry, who's standing beside me.

'Yeah,' he says. 'It's probably a sturgeon.'

Whatever it was is gone in the blink of an eye. 'That big?'

'Sure,' he says. 'I've seen them over a hundred pounds. They can thrash a net to pieces if they get caught in it.'

Don and Mike finish talking and Don goes back up to the wheelhouse. Soon the Enterprise is moving again and I forget about the shadow in the water.

When we come into the wharf, Dylan is waiting with the forklift. He says he wants to talk to me, so as soon as the Enterprise is berthed I cycle over to the plant.

'I want to show you something,' he says as I follow him back to his locker.

The first thing I notice when he opens the grey metal door is a puddle of water on the floor. Then I look up and see a waterlogged backpack hanging from the hook.

'Isn't that Cruddy's?' I ask.

'I thought it was, but I wanted to be sure.'

He takes it off the hook and unzips the pockets. There's nothing inside.

'Where did you find it?'

'It was in the harbour, slapping against the wharf.'

Dylan turns the backpack over to Tim, who calls the police. I don't wait until they get there because I don't know anything about it. Instead, I go home and clean out the pool.

The sun feels good on my back as I skim out the bugs and grass. I'm just finishing up when Mom comes out with a tray of hamburg patties and asks me to start the barbecue. I look at my watch. 'Is Dad finished already?'

'Yep. A water pipe blew and flooded the operating rooms so they had to shut down.'

She arranges silverware and napkins on the patio table before bringing out potato salad and sliced tomatoes. Pretty soon Dad comes out of the house carrying a beer, not looking the least bit upset about being home early. He looks at the barbecue and says, 'Can you hold off on those burgers while I take a swim?'

'Sure.'

I watch him swim a few laps of backstroke before he spreads himself out like a beetle and floats. As soon as he gets out and starts drying himself off I put the burgers on the grill.

Mom and Dad serve themselves before I help myself to the food. I wolf down everything on my plate and then go back for seconds. Chocolate cake and ice cream finish me off.

Dad and I are in what Mom calls a state of détente, which is basically a time-out for grownups. I tell him about Dylan finding

Cruddy's backpack in the harbour and he looks puzzled. 'I thought his car was found near the Point? Didn't they have the divers out there?'

'Yeah. They thought he might be in the water.'

'But they didn't find anything,' Mom says.

Dad turns his attention to her. 'Where did you hear that?'

'Euta told me when I was in the post office.' (Euta is the town's undisputed know-it-all.) 'She said not to say anything, so keep it quiet.'

Dad shakes his head. 'She told you this in the post office and she wants *you* to keep it quiet?'

Mom shrugs. 'Does anyone want coffee?'

Al calls after dinner and we talk about how Cruddy's backpack could have ended up in the harbour when his car was found miles away near the Point.

'It could have fallen off him and drifted down with the current,' I suggest.

'Except for one important detail,' he says.

'What's that?'

'The current flows the other way.'

'Oh yeah.'

'One thing's for certain,' he says. 'Cruddy's not being looked at as a runaway anymore. When the police came this time they were a lot different.'

'What do you think we should do?' I ask.

'What do you mean?'

'I mean, should we look for him?'

'I'd look,' Al says, 'if I knew where to look.'

No sooner does Al hang up than Lacey's at the door in her Speedo. Mom intercepts her in the kitchen and loads her up with a plate of potato salad in case she's hungry after her swim. Lacey thanks her and says hello to Dad from the door of his study. He waves to her without looking up from his papers.

Lacey doesn't waste any time getting into the pool. She glides through the water like a seal. I do a few laps of breaststroke before switching to the butterfly. Lacey doesn't like that because it churns up the pool.

'I'm drowning here, Andy,' she shouts. 'Knock it off!'

I grin at her and keep it up.

'Okay, fish boy, you're going down!'

Before I know it we're neck and neck, flipping at the pool edge and flinging our arms over our heads. Fortunately for me, the butterfly is the one stroke she can't defeat me in.

'Giving up already?' I say as she pulls herself out of the pool.

She points to her stomach. 'Hungry!'

I scoop up a handful of water and fling it at her retreating back, then I get out and dry myself off.

'Would you like something to drink?' I ask. 'A Pepsi, maybe?'

'Okay.'

'Diet or regular?'

She gives me a pained look and says, 'Diet, of course. Do you know how many calories are in the regular?'

Yeah, yeah, yeah.

When we've settled into our lounge chairs Lacey takes a sip of her drink and says, 'What's the latest on Cruddy?'

I tell her about Dylan finding his backpack in the harbour.

'You know what, Andy? I think he's dead.'

This is the first time I've heard anyone say this out loud.

'You do? Why?'

She takes another sip and puts down the can. 'Doesn't his name ring a bell? Sewell? Malcolm Sewell?'

I look at her dumbly. I'm not getting it.

'Think back a couple of years. This isn't the first time one of the Sewells has gone missing.'

I wrack my brain and eventually come up with a name. Gary.

'That's right. Gary Sewell. Remember, his house caught fire and the firemen discovered a grow-op in the basement?'

'That was Cruddy's house?'

'Yeah, and Gary Sewell was his father. And two days after the house burnt down, he disappeared.'

I think about the implications. 'Do you think that has something to do with Cruddy's disappearance?'

'I don't know,' she says. 'But there's a lot of bad people in that business.'

CHAPTER 11

The next day the police divers are all over the harbour. I'm beginning to wonder if Lacey's right and Cruddy *is* dead.

It's one o'clock when we finish unloading the Enterprise. The divers have just finished their search and are peeling off their masks. They talk, heads nod, heads shake, heads nod again. A vision of Cruddy, his fish-white face bloated twice its size and his eyes popping out of his head, takes hold in my brain and I feel sick.

A few minutes later they all take off, so I know they haven't found anything. They've searched the water where his car was found and they've searched the harbour where his backpack was found. Where the hell is he?

I think about all of this as I pedal to the gym, and the truth is, I can't come up with anything. Obviously Cruddy hasn't shown up at any of his usual haunts or the police would have known.

As I'm pedalling through the stop sign at the top of the hill a thought comes to me: What if Cruddy thought someone bad was after him? Did he leave his car between the two cottages on purpose, to make it look like he drowned?

This leads to another thought: If that's what happened, how did Cruddy get away? Was someone helping him?

Cruddy having an accomplice is a comforting thought, because if Cruddy had an accomplice, he probably drove him somewhere safe.

I decide to believe this is what happened, not that Cruddy went swimming and drowned, or was murdered by dope dealers. Maybe I just need a story I can live with, because the thought that I turned him away when he asked me for money, when I could have taken it out of my savings or borrowed it from Lacey, is pretty hard to take. It feels better to believe that he's okay, that *someone* out there helped him.

I go back to the routine of my life believing this.

CHAPTER 12

One day an OPP patrol boat pulls alongside the Enterprise and a couple of officers board us. We're not surprised to be boarded, but we're surprised it's the OPP. We're subject to inspections from the U.S. Customs agents patrolling the watery line separating Canada and the United States - that's a matter of territory. And it's not unusual to have impromptu visits from the Ministry of Natural Resources - that's a matter of fish quotas. But the OPP? The OPP normally check pleasure boats for lifejackets and booze, not search fishing vessels. They ask to look at the nets we've brought up and the catch that's in the totes.

Digging through the totes isn't easy. We end up shovelling the fish and ice into smaller bins, then shovel it back into the totes. Eventually the officers go down to the engine room and when they're finished there they head up to the wheelhouse. They have a short conversation with Don, then leave.

As soon as their boat pulls away Don tells us they're looking for drugs. The only drug I've seen on the Enterprise is a bottle of Tylenol, but, of course, that's not the kind they're looking for.

'Did you ask them what *they've* been smokin'?' Larry says.

Everyone has a good laugh over this, but the truth is that the mood on deck changes.

Scottie shakes his head. 'I don't know about this "war on drugs" thing. If it is a war, it seems to me it's another Vietnam. Long and hopeless.'

'It's like Prohibition,' Mike says. 'When *booze* was illegal in the 1920s it was taken over by gangs like Al Capone's. That's what it's like with drugs now.'

'You know, using fishermen to smuggle drugs isn't that farfetched,' Larry adds. 'The rumrunners working the lake used fishing tugs to get booze across.'

'Yeah, but they didn't have the drones watching them all the time,' Scottie says. 'There's no way you could do a straight hand-off between boats the way they did.'

'You should write a poem about it,' Mike says.

Scottie considers this and says, 'You know, I just might.'

I'm surprised. 'You write poetry, Scottie?'

'Does he write poetry?' Mike says. 'He's a regular Walt Whitman.'

'Got to do something in the off hours,' Scottie replies.

'What do you write about?'

'All this,' he says, sweeping his hand over the boat and the water. 'Poetry is my passion. What's yours?'

I stare at him blankly, so he continues.

'Given your background, I'd say your life has been mostly about achievement, hasn't it? Getting the best grades, being the best son?'

He's incredibly accurate.

'But I think you're switching gears, which is good. A lot of people never examine their core, until they crash. Then they *have* to look at it before they can move on.'

'Is that what happened to you?' I ask. 'You crashed?'

'Oh yeah, big time. It doesn't matter how. Everyone has their own way.'

I think about what Scottie's said as we plow through the lake on our way home. Maybe it's a burning passion inside of me that makes me want to fish. I don't know. Maybe it's just that I like the life.

CHAPTER 13

Before we get off the tug Don tells us we'll be going to Port Stanley soon. Port Stanley is northeast, two hours away by car. I haven't the faintest idea how I'm going to get there.

'We don't commute,' Mike explains. 'We live there. There's a berth reserved for the Enterprise and we move the whole operation up there.'

'But why?'

'Because Don's quotas are spread over three counties. Port Stanley is in Elgin County and he's doing it next. It's nothing to worry about, Andy. Port Stanley is a nice little port.'

I wasn't expecting this, and a million things run through my mind. 'When do we come back?'

'Sometime in August,' he says.

'August!'

'Yeah, August. Why? Is there someplace you've got to be?'

I don't want him to think I'm not cut out for the job so I tell him it's no problem. 'Do we sleep on the boat?' I ask.

'No, no. Don rents a house for us. You should get ready though because we could be off at a moment's notice.'

I tell Mom about it when I get home. She smiles and says, 'I guess you'll have to get your own meals while you're up there. You can do that.'

'But I won't have a car.'

'You don't need a car. The wharf's right in town and you can walk everywhere.'

Lacey is thrilled when I tell her. 'You'll have a great time, Andy.'

'I will?' I'm not so sure.

We're eating ice cream cones at her place in between an eyebrow wax and a cut-and-blow dry. The aroma of shampoo and mousse wafts out to the back porch.

'Maybe I could drive up sometime and we could go to the beach,' she says.

'I don't know if it has a beach.'

'Of course it has a beach. Everyone hangs out there. Stop pouting like your parents are sending you off to summer camp.'

It's scary how she can pinpoint my moods like that.

'Listen, I've got something for you,' she says. 'You know that eyebrow wax I just did?'

'Yeah.'

'Well, it turns out the lady is a good friend of Cruddy's mother. She actually took her in after her house burnt down.' She licks the ice cream running down her cone. 'Anyway, that's not the important part.'

'What's the important part?'

'The important part is that her niece comes down from Tilbury to visit her quite often.'

'So?'

'So, she was down the day Cruddy disappeared.'

My face must register the fact that I'm not getting it.

'Cruddy had a *crush* on her, Andy.'

I think this over, and for the life of me I can't picture Cruddy with a girl. I thought girls would scare him.

Lacey continues. 'Anyway, the niece agreed to go out with Cruddy that night. He was supposed to take her to Burger King for dinner.

But you know what? He stood her up. What would make a guy like Cruddy, who's got a crush on a girl, stand her up?'

Right then I realize that Cruddy asked me for money because he had a date. I bury my face in my hands and groan. Lacey asks me what's the matter and I tell her.

'Jeez,' I say when I look up, 'if only he'd told me. I just couldn't get him to talk to me.'

She puts a hand on my shoulder. 'He probably asked her out on impulse. It doesn't explain why he disappeared.'

'You don't think so?'

'No. Skipping out on a date is one thing. Disappearing from the face of the earth is quite another.'

'Yeah, and Cruddy wouldn't leave his job. It's basically all he has.'

'Well, he's got his mother, but she's not much better off than he is.'

I think out loud for a minute. 'Okay, so Cruddy asks me for money …'

'Which you don't give him.'

I roll my eyes. 'Thanks. I'm just saying that if he couldn't get it from me, and his mother couldn't help him out, what would he do?'

Lacey considers this, then replies, 'If he was really gaga about the girl and couldn't think of another way, he might try to steal it.'

A list of all the places Cruddy could steal money from runs through my mind. The plant? Not likely. Everyone's got a padlock on their locker and the petty cash is kept under lock and key in the office.

'Well, he didn't take down a convenience store or the police would have heard about it,' I say.

'True. Unless it wasn't a *legal* business. In which case, they couldn't really run to the cops, could they?'

'We're back to the drug trade again, aren't we?'

'Well, Cruddy has ties to that world. Even if he isn't part of it, he knows who is. And, it's a cash business. Maybe he took a chance.'

'I don't know, Lacey. If he stole the money from some druggie, why didn't he keep his date at Burger King?'

She thinks for a minute. 'Maybe he got caught.'

'By whom? I don't know anyone in that world.'

'Sure you do,' she says.

'I do?'

'Yeah, you know Sean Mullen. Remember a couple of years ago in the boys' washroom - Mr. Mallender reaching between his legs and catching his stash just before it went down the toilet?'

I look at her in amazement. 'I didn't know about that.'

She arches an eyebrow. 'How could you not know? The whole school knew.'

'I must have been sitting at the wrong lunch table that day.'

'I guess.'

'You mean, Sean was dealing?'

'Duh, that's why you never saw him after the tenth grade.'

'You think Cruddy went to Sean?'

She sighs in exasperation. 'I have no idea, Andy. I'm just saying that you're not as distant from the drug scene as you think. It's everywhere. Even in your remote corner of the world.'

Just then a car drives up and whatever I'm about to say is cut short by the appearance of Lacey's cut-and-blow dry.

CHAPTER 14

The lake is so rough the next morning that I upchuck my breakfast. 'Always a good idea to do that downwind,' Scottie says, too late.

This is the roughest weather I've experienced since I started. Half an hour earlier Don was debating whether or not to leave port. At 4:00 a.m. the winds were clocking 55 knots, but they pulled back to 40 and he decided to head out.

'Have you ever been out in 55?' I ask Scottie.

'Once,' he says. 'We were out near the Sisters when a storm blew up out of nowhere. Biggest waves I've ever seen.'

'How did you get out of it?'

'Don got us into Scudder Marina on the island and we waited it out.'

Larry chuckles. 'Remember Phil running up to the wheelhouse and throwing down the survival suits? I've never seen him so motivated.'

'Who's Phil?'

'The guy you're replacing,' Larry says. 'Something's wrong with his back.'

'Don said he might be off for a couple of months.'

'Might be off entirely,' Scottie says. 'You blow one of those discs and it can put you right out of commission. But you seem all right. I don't think Don would have a problem keeping you on.'

Don thinks I'm doing a good job! This is all the incentive I need to get my own gear, so Lacey and I take a drive to the Net and Twine store in Wheatley. We're not in the car more than five minutes before I realize she's in a temper. 'What's eating you?' I ask.

'That wiener, Dexter,' she replies.

As she turns onto the concession road I say, 'As in, Dexter, the boyfriend?'

Her scowl tells me that Dexter has worked his way over to the bad side.

'What did he do?'

Her eyes flare. 'You know what those self-important football jackasses are like!'

'Could you be more specific?'

'It's this whole question of entitlement,' she says, as though I know what she's talking about.

'Entitlement to what?'

She turns and gives me a look. 'To this,' she says, sweeping her hand over her body.

'Oh.'

'They think they're doing you such a favour by going out with you that they expect dessert right off the bat. You know what I mean?'

Absolutely. At one point, I'd been after that dessert myself - and got an elbow in the gut for my trouble.

'I mean, how dense does Dexter think I am?' she sputters.

'Maybe football players are just hornier than most guys,' I offer weakly.

'No, Andy, it's not that they're *hornier*. It's that they're more deluded!'

'So, what did you tell him?'

'I told him that it's not the guy who decides when dessert's going to be served.'

I can guess how that went over.

'And do you know what that ignoramus had to say?'

Pretty much, yep.

'He said that if I didn't want to do "it" —
you see it's just an "it" to him — there were
plenty of girls who would.'

Stupid Dexter.

'So I told that scumbag he could just go find
himself one of those girls because we were
through.'

Lacey is out of breath and beet-red with
fury. I, on the other hand, am giddy with joy.
But I cover it by putting on my best "oh, that's
awful" face and offer my sincerest sympathy.

CHAPTER 15

It's over a hundred degrees on the water the next day and we're sweating buckets under our oil skins. It's a relief when we arrive back in port. Al is smoking outside the plant and Dylan is picking up the totes lined up on the wharf. I tell them to come over to my house for a swim when they get off work. They look at each other and snort, like I'm joking.

'Really, guys. Come over and cool off. I'll put some burgers on the barbie. It'll just be us.'

'Can I bring Boz?' Dylan asks.

'Sure.'

Dylan and Boz are in the pool playing Frisbee when Al shows up in a brand-new pair of swim trunks. 'Wow,' he says, 'you live in a mansion.'

'I guess it is. I've never lived anyplace else.'

'That's not true,' Dylan yells.

'Oh yeah. Except for Dylan's.'

'Slumming,' he says as he throws a long one to Boz. 'No wonder you came home.'

'That's not the reason.'

By the time we sit down to eat it's 4:30 and we're all starved. Naturally we get around to the subject of Cruddy.

'At least I know why Cruddy asked me for money that day,' I tell them.

Al stops his burger an inch from his mouth and says, 'You do?'

'Yeah, he had a date.'

He snickers. 'Cruddy had a date?'

'Yeah, I know it's hard to believe, but it's true. He was going to take a girl out for dinner but he didn't have the money.'

'No shit. I didn't think he had it in him.'

'I didn't either. I'm just sorry I didn't have anything to give him. I'm afraid he might have done something stupid to get it.'

Dylan looks skeptical. 'Steal it, you mean?'

'It's possible. What if he knew someone with a lot of cash sitting around, maybe somebody in the drug business?'

'Like who?' Dylan says.

'I can take a guess,' Al says, bitterly. 'Tanner.'

Dylan throws his head back in shock. 'Are you kidding me?'

Al gives him a stony look. 'No, I'm not kidding you.'

I'm bewildered. 'Who's Tanner?'

'He's the captain of the Bonnie Belle,' Dylan answers. He looks back at Al. 'Seriously?

You think Tanner's mixed up in the drug business?'

Al's voice develops an edge. 'On a scale of one to ten, I'd give it a 10.5.'

'Why?'

'You remember when the fish quotas first came in? There were eight tugs fishing out of the harbour before the quotas. Only four survived. Don had the money to buy in, but Tanner was one of the ones who didn't.'

'You're saying that Tanner pays for his quotas by running drugs?' Dylan says. 'You'd better be careful with talk like that.'

Al snarls at him. 'I said I was guessing. But it's a damned good guess. The first thing he did when the quotas came in was fire his men and replace them with a bunch of lowlifes who didn't know the first thing about fishing.'

'How do you know that?' I ask.

'My dad was one of the men he let go, and with most of the tugs going out of business, he couldn't get hired on anywhere else.'

I sit back and take a sip of my Coke. Now I understand why Al thinks the captain is a bad one.

'If you're right and Cruddy was stealing from Tanner, what do you think he'd do to him?'

Al looks at me like I'm the stupidest person alive. 'What do you think he'd do to him?'

Mom gets home as I'm shoving plates into the dishwasher. 'Turn on the TV!' she yells, but she gets the news channel up before I can even turn around. As soon as I see the screen, I freeze. There, strapped to a stretcher in front of an ambulance, is a body bag.

As it turns out, while Dylan and Al and I were swimming and eating burgers around the pool, the Geary family from Indiana was enjoying an afternoon at the Point. Mrs. Geary, the best swimmer of the group, had swum out into the lake. She was turning around, heading back to shore, when her hand hit something solid under the surface of the water. She thought it was a piece of driftwood in her way.

Mr. Geary was sitting at the water's edge building sandcastles with the kids, listening to their shrieks of laughter as the waves came in and demolished them. As soon as he heard his wife scream he sat the kids down at a picnic table and plunged in after her.

And that's how Cruddy's body was discovered.

CHAPTER 16

The minute Cruddy's body is found, the mood in our house changes. Even though the police haven't released the cause of death and there's been no mention of the drug trade, everything becomes more serious.

And it isn't just in our house. The whole town is stunned. Gossip starts flying: that Cruddy was just like his father, that the fruit doesn't fall far from the tree - that sort of thing.

A couple of days later Mom meets me when I get home from work. She wants to have a talk. Something inside me bristles.

She pours some iced tea and we sit at the kitchen table. Before she gets started she holds up her hand and says, 'Hear me out before you say anything.'

The moment I've been dreading has arrived. Mom has switched sides.

'Andy, your father … your father and I … think you seriously need to reconsider your options.' I'm about to interrupt when she shushes me. 'Let me speak, please.'

I nod and let her carry on.

'You're very young and your life is going to turn on the decisions you make now. It may be that this fishing thing is the way to go, I don't know. But, maybe it isn't and you'll be throwing away some important opportunities. Acceptances from universities like Queen's won't always be there.'

'What's this all about, Mom? You were all for it in the beginning.'

'It's just, well … we'd like you to think about what you'd be giving up.'

I know what this is really about, so I say, 'Okay.'

She's surprised. 'Okay what?'

'Okay, I'll think about it.'

She eyes me suspiciously, as though it came out of my mouth too easily. And it did, because I know this isn't about whether I become a doctor or a fisherman. Somebody connected with the fishing industry, somebody I worked with, is dead. She's scared. To a certain extent, so am I. It's like the time a kid at school committed suicide. It took a long time for everyone to shake it.

'I still want you to be happy,' she adds. 'Both your father and I want that. We just want you to reconsider. Picture yourself at sixty-five, looking back on your life. Would you be looking back with regrets?'

All I can think is, you've got to be kidding me. Who can pretend they're sixty-five?

~

Al and Dylan and I are in the twilight zone. We can't figure out how it all played out, and neither, apparently, can the police. Nothing adds up.

'He must have gone swimming at the cottages and drowned,' Al says.

Dylan disagrees. 'Didn't you guys ever see the movie *Castaway*? The one with Tom Hanks?'

'Yeah,' I say. 'What about it?'

'Remember how he tried to launch a raft so that he could get back to civilization but the waves kept pushing it back to shore?'

'Yeah. He ended up rigging a sail, didn't he?'

'Right. Because he had to overcome the waves to get out to sea.'

'What are you saying?'

'I'm saying that if Cruddy drowned at the cottages, the waves would have pushed his body back against the breakwall. He wouldn't have been far enough out to float down to the Point.'

'I can't stand thinking about it,' Al says.

Dylan and I feel the same way, but we all know we won't be able to think of anything else.

CHAPTER 17

It's so blisteringly hot on the lake, the horizon is just a blur.

'Here,' Scottie says, digging out a scoop of crushed ice from one of the totes. 'You look like you're going to pass out.'

I press the ice to my face and start to revive.

Don cuts the engines as we reach our nets. The next minute he's down on deck with us, saying, 'Andy, go up to the wheelhouse for a bit.'

'What?' I say, stunned. 'What do you want me to do?'

'Don't do anything. Just sit there.'

I wonder what's going on as I mount the narrow stairs. It isn't until I'm perched in Don's chair that I see we're about twenty feet off the Bonnie Belle's port bow. I can see straight into the wheelhouse and it's empty. Pretty soon I hear harsh words passing across the boat decks and figure it has something to do with the Bonnie Belle putting its nets over ours.

I look around the wheelhouse uneasily, wondering what to do if the radio cackles alive. There's radar, sonar, computer screens, a GPS, and other navigational gizmos I know nothing about. What I do know is that the survival suits and life jackets are stored in the compartment beneath the mattresses and there's an inflatable life raft on the roof.

Suddenly, something catches my eye on the Bonnie Belle. A man wearing oil skins is bringing a package into the wheelhouse. He goes directly to the compartment behind the captain's chair and pulls out a life jacket. I'm wondering what the life jacket's for when he grabs hold of the material and rips open the seam. That's when I have the uneasy feeling that I'm not supposed to be seeing this. He takes the package he's holding and shoves it in where the stuffing should be, then closes the seam again.

I'm frozen in place, barely breathing. I watch him close the door to the compartment and start back down the stairs. Then, inexplicably, he looks up, straight into my eyes. As soon as he recovers from the shock of seeing me he puts his finger to his lips in that universal symbol of "keep quiet if you know what's good for you", and, just in case I didn't get his meaning, runs the same finger across his throat. My stomach sours but I look off in another direction, pretending I don't have the foggiest idea what he's on about. When I look back, he's gone.

After Don finishes telling off Captain Tanner, he joins me in the wheelhouse. I'm weighing the threat the guy's made, not sure if I should tell Don and get him involved. I'm just about to open my mouth when a huge, honking flock of Canada geese flies over and drowns everything out. I see it as a sign and go quietly back to the boat deck to help haul in the nets.

CHAPTER 18

By the time I get to the gym, the morning crowd has left and I have the weight room all to myself. I'm warming up when Wendell and Dexter come in. One look at them tells me I'm in trouble.

'Oh look,' Wendell says to Dexter, 'it's the fish boy.'

There's no mistaking the sinister quality in his voice. He looks around the room as if he doesn't know it's empty and says, 'Too bad your girlfriend's not here to stand up for you.'

'Funny,' I say, in an effort to wipe the smirk off Dexter's face, 'I thought she was *his* girlfriend.'

Dexter's lips tighten and his fists clench. 'Why you …' he sputters.

So, here I am with the two football boys: Wendell looking for payback for Lacey cutting him down the other day, and Dexter pissed because she dumped him, and I'm thinking about what's going to happen next and how I sure do take it on the chin for that girl, when a couple of old guys walk into the room. Wendell and Dexter back off because any funny business and Wendell will lose his job. 'I guess we'll see you around,' he says, menacingly.

I want to make some smart remark but manage to hold my tongue.

I finish the rest of my workout, thinking I'm in the clear, only to discover Wendell and Dexter waiting for me in the locker room. Other people are around so the best they can do is smirk at me like I'm a dead man walking.

It isn't until I've showered and changed and out in the parking lot that I realize my bike is gone. This gets me so ripped that I storm back into the building and tell Wendell and Dexter in the loudest possible terms what losers they are for stealing my bike.

Dexter trades looks with Wendell and says, in a singsong voice, 'Did we steal fish boy's bike, Wendell?'

Wendell pretends to be thinking - a big stretch for him.

'I don't think so. What's it look like?'

'You know perfectly well what it looks like, you thieving bastards!'

Wendell wags his finger at me. 'No, no, Andy. Swearing's not allowed in the club. You can get your membership revoked for that.'

'Go to hell, Wendell,' I spit out as I storm out of the locker room.

CHAPTER 19

I call it "The Big Gap": the time between when I lost consciousness and when I woke up in a Search and Rescue helicopter. It wasn't until the trial that I got a complete picture of what else happened that day.

What I do remember is Lacey pushing her way into the ER cubicle I was lying in. Later I discovered they'd let her in because she was pitching a fit in the waiting room. Dexter and Wendell were there too. I wondered if that meant the big romance was back on, but it wasn't.

Apparently, after I'd accused Dexter and Wendell of stealing my bike, they followed me out of the locker room, spitting mad and itching for a fight. They arrived at the front door of the gym just as two guys were throwing me into a white van. Even to them that seemed a bit off, so they gave chase.

At the same time, Lacey was coming in for her steam and wondered what the heck Dexter and Wendell were doing running through the parking lot. They flagged her down and jumped in her car. Then they held on for dear life as she split out of the parking lot like a bat out of hell. She almost smacked head-on into a Handi-Transit bus as she swung around a lineup of cars turning into the Tim Hortons drive thru, all the while screaming at Dexter to take down the licence plate number of the van and call it in. They played the 911 call in court. It sounded something like this:

Operator: Police, fire, or ambulance?

Dexter: Ah … police.

Operator: What is your emergency?

Dexter: Um … well … you see … my friend … well he's not exactly my friend … he was …

Lacey: (screaming at him) Dexter, you idiot! Give me that phone! (Rustling sounds)

Operator: What is the nature of your emergency?

Lacey: My friend just got grabbed in the parking lot of the fitness club!

Operator: Do you think he was taken against his will?

Lacey: Of course it was against his will!

Operator: Are you sure?

Lacey: (testy) Yes! I've got two eyewitnesses in the car with me! It's a big white van.

Dexter (in the background): A Ford cube van.

Lacey: A Ford cube van. The license plate number is … what is it, Dexter? (Dexter mumbling in the background) … AGHT 503. I'm trying to follow it but it's getting away.

Operator: Where are you?

Lacey: I'm driving east on Lake Drive. I've just passed the Albuna Town Line.

Operator: What is your name, Miss?

Lacey: Pardon?

Operator: What is your name?

Lacey: (frustrated) What difference does it make what my name is? Get this on dispatch! Do you have any idea how small your window is in a kidnapping? (She told me later she got this off TV.)

Operator: A car has been dispatched, Miss. Please calm down.

Lacey: (furious) *A* CAR? WHAT DO YOU MEAN *A* CAR? THIS IS AN ALL-HANDS-ON-DECK, DROP-WHATEVER-YOU'RE-

DOING 911 CALL! THIS IS DOCTOR TOWELL'S SON, ANDY TOWELL! HE'S JUST BEEN KIDNAPPED! WHAT MORE DO YOU NEED?

Operator: One moment, Miss. Please stay on the line.

Lacey: (huffing and puffing) Here, you deal with her, Dexter!

(Sound of the car engine revving up and several horns going off.)

Dexter: Ah … hello … are you still there?

No need to repeat the rest. Suffice to say that within minutes Lacey's car was passed by a convoy of screaming police cars.

And still they lost the van.

Lacey told me the rest later, how she'd driven down every little side road along the lake until she spotted a sliver of the van through a crack in a fence. She grabbed the phone from Dexter and screamed at the operator: GET

THE SEARCH AND RESCUE HELICOPTER UP! THEY'RE GOING TO KILL HIM ON THE LAKE! (She didn't know that, of course, but she figured I was going to be the next Cruddy. Fortunately for me, the Coast Guard helicopter was on a training exercise two miles away.)

And that's how Lacey saved my life. The helicopter got to the Bonnie Belle just as my limp body was being transferred from a motorboat. At that point the crew realized the jig was up and raised their hands over their heads.

CHAPTER 20

Lacey was right about Cruddy being killed on the lake. The police got one of the crew to crack in return for a reduced sentence. He told them that Cruddy hadn't been stealing from Tanner. He'd just been in the wrong place at the wrong time.

It was the day I'd forgotten my gym bag and had to go back to the plant to get it. Cruddy had finished his shift and was walking to his car when he accidentally witnessed the hand-off of that day's stash from the Bonnie Belle to the men in the white van. And that was the beginning of the end for him.

After they got him on board the tug, they drugged him and dumped him into one of the totes filled with crushed ice. Then, when it was dark, they took the boat out into the lake to dump him. One of the other scumbags drove Cruddy's car to the cottages near the Point and left it there. The white van picked him up and they drove off.

Ironically, the Bonnie Belle ran into one of the Ministry's boats on its way out of the harbour. Tanner made up some excuse about forgetting to drop one of his nets and they waved him on. When they were far offshore, the crew tied Cruddy by his shirt to one of the anchors and sent him to the bottom of the lake. Then they sped away. Just as cruel and heartless as that. Not knowing, or caring, if he was still alive. And, unlike Dylan, South Bay Bessie didn't save Cruddy.

Al had been right, too. The Crown estimated that over the years Captain Tanner had smuggled in millions of dollars of illegal and prescription drugs from the U.S.. An American yacht would carry the packages as close to the international border as possible then have a diver attach them to the Bonnie Belle's nets.

Of course, to pull it off Tanner had to have the co-operation of all his men. Getting everyone to turn into drug smugglers would have been impossible, so he fired his crew, which included Al's father, and started fresh with people provided through his criminal contacts. They hid the drugs in the life jackets until the men in the white van picked them up. Normally they made the transfer in the dead of night, but the cops had been patrolling more regularly, so they did it in broad daylight. And that change in schedule proved fatal for Cruddy.

If there hadn't been a murder and an attempted murder charge, Tanner's lawyer might have been able to negotiate a decent sentence for him. As it was, Drug Enforcement had seized the Bonnie Belle so his fishing days were over anyway. From now on, the only thing he'll be sailing around is his prison sink.

Life turns on a series of 'ifs' sometimes:

If the police hadn't started regular night patrols at the dock …

If Cruddy hadn't parked his car in front of the Bonnie Belle that day …

If I hadn't been distracted by the freighter and noticed the white van parked by the Bonnie Belle's berth …

I wonder if Cruddy saw me careening down the hill as the goons loaded him onto the tug. Did he throw his backpack in the water to get my attention? Was that the splash I'd heard? I wish I could ask him. I wish I could tell him I'm sorry for what happened.

Then there's Mom and Dad. Mom was at home when the **OPP** officer came to the door. When she saw him she thought Dad had been in a car accident. When she learned what was really going on, she was horrified. She called Dad and he rushed right home. The police were careful not to give them any false hope but Mom says they were able to figure out the odds for themselves.

While they were sitting at home fretting, they got a call from Lacey saying she'd found the van but that it was empty. At that moment Dexter and Wendell were kicking in the door of the cottage, which was being used as a drug sorting and distribution centre. It, too, was empty.

The 911 operator told Lacey to get on the dock and wave something so that the Coast Guard helicopter could pinpoint her location. As soon as she heard it coming, she stripped out of her shirt and waved it frantically over her head. When the pilot saw her, he made a 90-degree turn out into the lake, with the **OPP** speedboat roaring up behind him.

Dexter and Wendell were on the dock too, pretending to wave as their eyeballs bugged out of their sockets.

CHAPTER 21

Don couldn't wait until everything was sorted out; he had to get the Enterprise to Port Stanley. But he told me to take some time off and if I still wanted to crew he'd have a spot for me.

Naturally, I thought Mom would be the most freaked out by my kidnapping, but it was really Dad. He likes to be in charge. Waiting around just isn't in his character. Neither is trusting that everyone knows their job and will do it well. Of course, Mom and Dad didn't know *why* I'd been taken so they were sitting at home expecting a ransom demand.

My biggest concern was that I'd be shipped off to university now, whether I liked it or not. But I couldn't have been more wrong. For some reason, Dad did a complete one-eighty.

'You don't understand that?' Lacey said.

'Not really.'

'Andy, imagine you had a kid, and that kid was taken from you. But, through some bizarre twist of fate, you got him back. Can you picture that?'

'I guess so.'

'Don't you think you'd be so grateful to have that living, breathing person back in your life that everything else would be fairly insignificant? Your dad's relieved, Andy, and he's backing off.'

That was so unlike Dad, I found it hard to believe.

Lacey and I were sitting side by side in the park by the beach. I'd casually draped my arm around her. She'd noticed but didn't object.

'So, what are you going to do now?' she asked.

I hadn't really thought it through so I didn't know what to say. Then I realized she was talking about something else.

'Your dad's leaving it up to you to decide, Andy.'

Her hair smelled nice.

'I have an idea,' she said. 'Do you want to hear it?'

The whole scene was intoxicating. The warm air, the way she smelled, the water stretching out in front of us.

'Ah huh,' I answered hazily.

'I think you should do both.'

'Do both of what?'

'Fish *and* get an education.'

'Yeah? How am I going to do that?'

'Take a degree online in your spare time. You've got to admit, Andy, you've got a lot of spare time.'

Her skin was smooth and warm underneath my hand.

She turned to see why I wasn't responding to her suggestion. The look on my face must have said it all.

She smiled and settled back in the bench. I ran my fingers over her shoulder and felt her surrender to the sensation.

Don't worry, I'm not going to make a move on her. Not until she realizes that she's madly, deeply in love with me.

Acknowledgments

I consider myself fortunate to live in a fishing port on the shores of Lake Erie. Up until March of 2012 my exposure to the fishing industry was limited to the fresh perch and pickerel I bought at the Kingsville dock. That changed when I met Don Rutgers, captain of the fishing tug 'William TR'. He introduced me to his fascinating world and generously provided the knowledge and technical expertise that formed the backdrop of this book.

My gratitude also extends to Tim Tiessen of La Nassa Foods for his invaluable tours of the assessment and processing plants, and his overview of the scaling, filleting, and packaging of the fish brought in by the tugs.

The inspiration for the fisherman/poet, Scottie, was provided by Mike Wilson of Port Stanley, who is featured in the documentary, 'Sea Without Tides' and along with Don and Tim shares a contagious enthusiasm for the commercial fishing industry on Lake Erie.

About The Author

Margaret J. McMaster published her first book of middle-grade fiction, **Carried Away on Licorice Days**, in 2008. It was nominated for three literary awards: the Canadian Library Association's Book of the Year for Children Award, the 2010/2011 Hackmatack Children's Choice Book Award, and the 2011 Rocky Mountain Book Award.

In 2009 she started writing the Babysitter Out of Control! series. These amusing, fast-paced adventures include: **Babysitter Out of Control!**, **Looking for Love on Mongo Tongo**, **The Improbable Party on Purple Plum Lane**, **What Happened in July** (a *Best Books for Kids & Teens* selection), **The Sinking of the Wiley Bean**, and, **The Queen of Second Chances**. **The Complete Babysitter Out of Control! Series**, published in 2015, was long-listed for the *2016 Silver Birch Award*, a *Best Books for Kids & Teens* selection, and won the Gold Medal in the *2015 Moonbeam Children's Book Award* Early Reader/1st Chapter Books category.

McMaster is a past contributor to the *Canadian Children's Annual* and her creative non-fiction piece, *After All These Years*, was shortlisted for the 2006 CBC Literary Award. *So Much Potential*, a novel set in the Lake Erie fishing industry, was a *Best Book for Kids & Teens* *Starred* Selection.

The first book in her Phoebe Sproule series, **8 Days in DUMBO**, was named one of *The Year's Best* by *Resource Links* and won an Honorable Mention in the *2019/2020 Reader Views Literary Awards*. The sequel, **The Haunting of Cedar Hill Plantation**, was released in 2020.

9 780981 052571